To Tim.

There Is a Balm in Gilead:

God's Healing Love, Grace and Compassion

A collection of short stories

by
Brian Reddish

Reddish Dec 2016

There Is a Balm in Gilead: God's Healing Grace
© 2015 by Brian Reddish
ISBN 978-0-9932747-6-3
Published by Caracal Books
United Kingdom www.caracalent.uk

Dedication

This book is dedicated to my dear wife,
Pauline,
who has sustained and kept me
through all these years.

Contents

Prologue   i

Calvary   1

Darjeeling Tea   9

The Cottage Flower   29

The Weeping Willow Tree   37

Edit the Tape   47

Epilogue   59

Prologue

Do you believe thoughts and pictures can be inspired by God? If so, you will appreciate along with me that this is exactly what occurred in these stories. Why should this have to be and for what purpose? A good question!

Let us give a particular scenario. If you saw a little child crying after falling down, or the expression of pain written across the face of an old lady struggling with arthritis in her legs whilst carrying shopping, would you feel anything within yourself and wish you could help somehow?

There would probably be two types of responses to these situations. One person might feel the situation required help, but would simply walk on by thinking, *Oh what a shame!* Another person, perhaps herself a mother of a child of similar age, would rush with immediate concern to help as if identifying herself personally with the child's need and pain and feeling it all the more because she has a child herself! Further, the struggling old lady would also be treated with practical passion and offered help in some way. Both people saw and felt the pain exhibited before them, but only the second was prepared to act outside the box without any sense of inconvenience, reserve or embarrassment.

Well, I believe God is like the second person. Remember the story Jesus told of The Good Samaritan? God has compassion*. It is part of His agape love towards each one, and this is all included in that Golden Rule: do to others as you would have them do to you!

There exists much pain and suffering in the world today. Each one of the stories in this book will take the reader into observing some of the needs of others. The reader must imagine for themselves what God might say or do to remedy these needs.

This is what I mean by having inspired thoughts and pictures. God seeks to choose people who will see as he sees, feel as He feels and act upon situations just as He would. If I say I love God, then I must learn to love what He loves – PEOPLE!

* Jesus was *"moved with compassion"* when observing people's needs. It was the direct motive for at least five of His miracles.

Calvary

"I have been sent to heal the broken hearted. To proclaim liberty to the captives and set free those who are bound…"

"And when they had come to the place called CALVARY, there they crucified HIM."
Luke 23:33

Calvary

Several figures stood before me. *Who were they?* Each one seemed heavily clothed. As they drew closer, I observed that, in fact, it was baggage they were carrying. Their baggage was mostly strapped to them upon their backs, but also around their waists. How strange! I was bemused!

As they drew closer and came into view, I was able to observe their countenance and facial expressions. Each one exhibited some degree of pain as if under the strain of carrying their loads.

Further, to add to their burden, there was another obstacle. They were walking through thick undergrowth of tall grass and prickly briars, which made their journey arduous. It was difficult for them to walk properly!

I wondered why they were carrying such heavy bags in the first place. *Why didn't they at least follow an easier path than the one they were taking?* Suddenly, my thoughts were interrupted by the sound of a dark voice, "They cannot remove their bags. See how they are so tight around them. They think their loads are part of their bodies! They have accepted this condition as their plight – something that they can never change. Each one is resigned to live with the load!"

"Who are you?" I asked the owner of the dark voice. "How do you know these things?"

"Ha... ha!" A hideous cry, which began to fade away like an echo, rang out. I heard a reply, "My name is memories."

I shouted very loudly with increasing curiosity, "What memories?"

By now, the voice had almost disappeared into the darkness from where it came, but an audible answer came resounding back saying, "Dark memories! Dark memories from the past – their pasts!"

In contrast, as soon as this dark episode finished, a bright light appeared, instantly extinguishing the darkness. At this interruption the figures standing before me lifted their heads gazing at the light, and then each one raised their hands as if beckoning for help. Their weary eyes seemed comforted. Their countenances glowed, reflecting the glory that shone upon them. In amazement I saw their straps break one by one as if they were made of straw, and all the figures were set free from their heavy loads!

What was happening? What was this Light? I heard the sound of a trumpet that seemed to summon me and prepare me to hear a message. *"I am the Light of the world,"* a voice spoke. *"I am the Word of God. I have come to bring good tidings to the poor. I have been sent to heal the broken-hearted. To proclaim liberty to the captives and set free those who are bound. To comfort those who mourn and give them the oil of joy for their sadness, a garment of praise instead of heaviness."* The voice that spoke was like the sound of many waters!

I asked the speaker about the figures. "Those bags they were carrying strapped upon each of their backs and around their waists... what were they?"

There was no answer. Instead, an interlude of complete silence followed, and then the scene changed. It became tranquil and serene like a sunset over an ocean. He spoke to me in a quiet voice. *"Each load they carried was created from past mistakes, hurts and difficulties that never received healing. As a result, their walk became weary with the weight of blaming themselves; regret, guilt and shame all rested heavily upon them."*

I enquired further of He who was called the *Word of God, the Light of the world* and asked Him what had caused these people to become transformed and free of their burdens? He spoke, somewhat surprised that I did not know the good news He was about to tell me, "Have you not known? Have you not heard that the everlasting God, the Lord, the Creator of the ends of the earth neither faints nor is weary? He gives power to the weak and to those who have no might He increases strength. He calls anyone to come to Him, those who labour and are heavy laden. He will set you free by His Truth and give you rest! There is a place called Calvary. Their loads and heavy burdens were lifted at Calvary."

After these things, the scene changed a second time. The night began to end as beams of light pierced it from the eastern skyline. From the womb of the morning the sun rose, giving birth to a new day!

Suddenly, the heavens opened before my eyes like a scroll being rolled apart. I saw what appeared to be gold dust that glittered beautifully as it fell into the radiant beams of sunlight. Out of the golden dust came flying creatures, filling the heavens! One of the creatures came near to me, blowing a long narrow trumpet held in one hand and pointing towards me with the other. Again I was being summoned to hear a message.

The one who had blown the trumpet looked towards me and spoke audibly saying, "Take heed and listen to Him, He that has spoken to you from Heaven. He is the Way, the Truth and the Life. No one comes to the Father but through Him! He is calling you by name! You shall know the Truth, and the Truth shall set you free!" After this, the creatures went back, as in a whirlwind, to Heaven. They were seen no more.

I now stood alone before the *Word of God, the Light of the world*. I felt weak and fell to my knees in His presence. "What must I do to be saved like those others?" I asked.

"Believe on the Son of God," He answered.

"Who is He that I might believe on Him?"

"You have seen Him, and it is He who is speaking to you," He replied.

"Lord, I believe!"

Suddenly, I heard joyous singing coming from Heaven. Looking upwards I heard one say, "There is joy in Heaven over one sinner who repents."

Another said, "This, my child was dead and is alive again; was lost and is found!"

Darjeeling Tea

James Gardner, along with his beautiful wife, Juliet, who was a couple of years younger than he was, had retired a few years before at the age of sixty. His working life had been in Further Education, teaching young people the delights of Mathematics, a subject he had loved. But his passion was equally in communicating its concepts to young people and helping and encouraging them. Juliet on the other hand had worked in several jobs; but like her husband, she had a wonderful way of communicating help, advice and encouragement to all she met in her own unique, kindly and generous manner.

James had always wanted to travel. It presented the opportunity, he thought, to see other lands and people, and as a consequence learn to see the bigger picture of human life! Whilst he believed that travelling would be an education, it did not follow that he had a craving for it. Both he and his wife were the kind of people to go through life closely together one step at a time with purpose, commitment and contentment. They had exhibited an enduring spirit through hard times with a patient kind of determination and resilience that saw them through many humble situations over the forty odd years of their marriage.

However, James and Juliet had now found the time and the means with which to travel, especially since their own three children had flown the nest a long time ago. A friend of theirs had recommended cruising the seas and stopping off at exotic ports around the world. "You must try it at least once," they had been advised.

And so it was in the month of December that they set sail on *The Enterprise*, heading for the Canaries. The whole experience of being at sea was exhilarating and magnificent!

As they sailed from Southampton and passed through the English Channel, James took note of how the depth of the sea was up to 200 metres or thereabouts. But on entering the Bay of Biscay and cruising into the Atlantic, he was amazed how the depth increased to 1800 metres! Around the ship were Information Monitors displaying the speed they were travelling at, together with various other bits of information such as their course, wind speed, their position in latitude and longitude and the depth of sea water.

James was sitting with his wife at a dining table admiring the sea view when he shared his enlightenment and intrigue over the depth of the sea with her. "I think my Geography teacher must have been right. The British Isles are in fact on a shelf of rock and were once joined to the mainland of France!"

This piece of interesting knowledge, that had so captured James, had not fully grabbed Juliet's attention in quite the same manner. In fact, quite suddenly, Juliet responded by asking a completely unrelated question, "What is the time?"

"About ten minutes to ten," replied James.

"I fancy going to a singing lesson. It starts at 10.00am in the Neptune Lounge."

"Do you really?" answered James, who was intrigued by Juliet's desire and impulse to sing.

"Yes. I spoke to a nice lady this morning, and she is going. Apparently, they teach you how to sing in harmony and other things. I'm quite excited about it!"

"That sounds great," said James, still somewhat taken by surprise but nevertheless pleased that his dear wife had found such an interest. Within a few seconds, James decided what he would do himself in his wife's absence. "I think maybe I will go to the gym for half an hour."

They parted with a kiss. "See you later," replied Juliet as she moved away excitedly towards the Neptune Lounge.

James thought so much about the wellbeing of Juliet that it always pleased him to see her doing something independently by herself. He had even suggested that it might be a good idea to make provision for a pension in her own name whilst she was working, thus enabling her to live more comfortably should he ever not be there for her. Further, when she had previously expressed a desire to do some voluntary work, James had encouraged her to follow it up, as he had with her interests at their local church. This way James saw his wife always being accomplished and fulfilled in the future.

No sooner had Juliet left to join the sopranos and altos and other "toes" than a middle-aged gentleman asked if he could sit and join James at his table. James immediately detected a Welsh accent and felt a warmth and friendliness about the man, who informed James that his name was Ryan Evans. The usual dialogue ensued, and the two men talked about the good food and how nice the cruise was. Then, the conversation moved on to enquiring about each other – where they came from, their respective occupations and the other's family life.

It was during the latter part of the conversation, as James spoke about his family life, when a change occurred. Ryan seemed uneasy, if not uncomfortable, as though James had pressed an unwelcome button in his life or experience. His speech slowed in pace; his voice altered to a soft and quiet tone. Looking straight at James, and with a serious gaze in his eyes, he gently said, "I have recently lost my wife."

Taken by surprise by Ryan's sudden declaration, James simply replied, "I am sorry to hear that."

Ryan went on to say how his wife, whose name had been Jenny, had suddenly been diagnosed with breast cancer – and within less than a year had passed away. Ryan and Jenny had been married fourteen years. Both were in their mid-forties and had two children. He had been advised by family members to come away on the cruise as was originally planned, thinking it would do him good.

Suddenly, on hearing these finer details, an atmosphere seemed to develop making the cruise and food and all of its enjoyment fade into insignificance. James again spoke to Ryan with even more earnestness, "I am so very sorry to hear that".

It was expedient for James to say very little at this moment; words were totally inadequate, though Ryan appeared comforted by James' efforts to console him by lending a listening ear.

Ryan continued further, "They told me I should go away on this cruise, but it is not helping at all. It does not matter where I go; I cannot be rid of this terrible pain inside my heart."

James could only try to imagine such pain. St Augustine's solemn thoughts, which seemed to relate to Ryan's experience very well, came to mind:

> *"Where was my heart to flee for refuge from my heart?*
> *Whither was I to fly where I would not follow?*
> *In what place should I not be prey to myself?"*

Some people do feel a little awkward or embarrassed talking to someone in such sad circumstances or when suddenly confronted with a person's tragic news. When greeted with the usual, "Good morning, and how are you?" one rarely receives a genuine heart-felt response to a reply involving a declaration of bad news! Rather, it seems more often than not that the atmosphere suddenly changes into an inhibited quietness, with a sense of awkwardness charging the air. To be fair, in such cases, ladies tend to respond more favourably and with better understanding than the men in these situations, especially regarding matters of the heart! Consequently, if a person happens to be suffering they can be made to feel all the more isolated and alone with seemingly no one to help or understand. Grief adds to grief. Happy conversations are the most palatable to people. Anything else approaching the truth regarding how one really feels is not what they wish to hear!

Whilst adverse reactions to sad news can affect some, how wonderful it is to be the recipient of those who can empathise with warm concern, understanding and compassion! In such cases, true is the saying, "A friend in need is a friend indeed!" Perhaps such a person has also suffered and finds it easier to offer help to those needing it, and yet one cannot help but think, *Have we not all experienced hardships of some kind at some time or another? They are common to man!*

Whatever the case, showing kindness, offering help, being thoughtful, generous and considerate of others – these are just a few selfless qualities which have their origin in that golden rule: "Do unto others as you would have them do to you." Surely against such there is no law! They cost nothing to exhibit yet always provide a wealth of consolation!

In reflecting upon these qualities, James immediately realised he should thank God. He thought, *I must thank God that I have such a wife in the person of Juliet, who exemplifies and demonstrates instant compassion upon all who are hurting or in need. She is the embodiment of kindness and goodness itself. Her unselfish nature and heart, as well as her lovely smile, attracts all who she happens to converse with for longer than a mere few seconds and makes them feel immediately at ease.* Of course, Juliet was his wife, and he would say such praise of her! Nevertheless, James had noticed this to be very true by other people's reactions and opinions and not just his own!

James remained quietly with Ryan as he sat motionless at the table. What could he say to him? He had come away hoping for some remedial help and consolation on the cruise, and had seemingly found none.

James decided to speak to Ryan again, and with a sympathetic voice, he said, "It must be very difficult for you." After a short pause, he went on to ask, "And how do you cope now?"

"It *is* very difficult," Ryan replied. Then, with his head partially bowed and staring distantly at some fictitious object upon the table as though studying it meticulously, he went on to say, "It is a loss that cannot be explained with words. You think to yourself, *How does life carry on?* To begin with you are in shock and busy doing lots of things. Then, after a week or so, when the funeral is over and family and friends have gone home, you begin to realise that Jenny is not coming back. Each day is an ordeal. Life is empty. Every day at least one previous conversation comes back to me… little things, like Jenny would often check me for being untidy and say something like, 'Ryan, why can't you leave your clothes tidy; there are hooks you know?' Now, I wish I could hear that reprimand from her again; it would be like music to my ears. I miss it!"

With these last words Ryan was clearly moved within himself so that his eyes revealed a pain far greater than words could express. It was as if deep within him was a hidden storehouse, holding many thoughts and emotions like a great reservoir full of fond memories and reflections of past times shared with his dear wife. Just one of these treasures had surfaced in his mind, and even an admonishment regarding untidiness had become a beautiful thing to him!

As James contemplated this, he was also deeply moved. *This was the kind of real love that pierces the heart,* he thought. Hearing all Ryan had just said brought home to James vividly and clearly just how much Ryan had loved his wife!

Conversation still seemed an intrusion to what Ryan was feeling. Throughout their discourse, he had continued to hold his head in the bowed position staring across the table. Putting his hands to his eyes he rubbed them gently, and as a consequence released a sudden discharge of teardrops that fell upon the table, as though they had been gathering for a long time and were now released. It was rather like a water tap that decides to send a small short continuous drip for a few seconds after it has been turned off. Instinctively, James placed his hand upon Ryan's shoulder and quietly asked him, "Can I get you anything? Would you like a cup of tea or coffee?"

"Tea would be nice," he replied. "That would be brilliant; thank you very much." Ryan reacted bravely, and playing down his feelings, he spoke to James in an unexpected positive manner, attempting to regain control. He went on to say, "Actually, I quite like the Darjeeling Tea in one of those sachets. Thanks! Thank you very much. That is kind of you."

It did not take long, and James soon returned with the tea Ryan had requested. James, too, had decided to try Ryan's favourite brand himself. It was a great feature of the cruise that drinks and eats were available at almost any time of day. "There you are, Ryan; Darjeeling Tea it is. I hope I didn't put too much milk in it. Darjeeling seems to be a light tea, and I noticed it only required the smallest amount of milk in order to whiten it. I think I put too much milk in mine."

"Thank you again," replied Ryan. "Yes, you are right; it is a very light tea indeed. Actually, I can drink this type of tea without any milk in it at all. It is very relaxing."

At this, James began to think to himself that perhaps Ryan may have preferred his tea without milk, so asked, "Oh, do you want me to get you another one without milk?"

"No, not at all," replied Ryan, suddenly recollecting what he had just said. Sensing he might have caused James to feel a little awkward and not wishing to sound finicky or ungrateful, he continued to say, "Sorry I said that, James. Please forgive me. I am very happy with the tea as it is. With milk is good. It is absolutely fine. Please do not worry; it is great."

For a moment, James felt as though Ryan was being a little over-apologetic, but then quite unexpectedly Ryan went on to say something that helped to shed light upon his sensitivity of the situation and gave James insight as to why he had perhaps reacted in the way he had. Ryan suddenly spoke about his wife, saying, "Jenny would always do the same thing and put milk in the tea. I would say to her that I preferred it without milk if it was Darjeeling. She would get confused, because if it was any other brand of tea, then I liked some milk in it, you see... except for Darjeeling Tea, then I liked it without milk.

"One time she got confused with my peculiar likes and dislikes when it came to having a cup of tea. I had asked her for a cup of Darjeeling Tea without milk, but she came back with the tea and had inadvertently put milk in it. Silly me! I was just about to point out the mistake, when she anticipated me and said abruptly, 'Ryan, next time you can get it yourself!'"

As James listened to Ryan recount this memory and observed his countenance when referring to his wife, the expression on Ryan's face clearly revealed that this recollection was very precious to him in spite of its nature! It was as if he would have been only too pleased to hear Jenny repeat those very same words of reproof! Ryan clearly had loved Jenny very much. This was vividly manifest in his reactions and sentiments towards her.

As Ryan recalled this memory of his late wife, James supposed there could well have been some degree of friction between them both at the time – and all over a simple cup of tea! Certainly, in some cases, other couples would have reacted in a very different manner, more adversely and with contrasting outcomes. James thought about how people today would consider ending a relationship over such trivialities as dirty loos, not replacing toilet rolls, leaving lights on, leaving dirty cups around the house, leaving wet towels on the floor, nagging about chores, overfilling bins, taking too long to get ready or simply flicking TV channels! How would the average couple respond in the scenario in which Ryan and Jenny were involved regarding the tea – better or worse?

A small flame can ignite a large fire when it touches dry straw, but in contrast the same flame when coming into contact with the fuse of a stick of dynamite would cause an explosion! Likewise, depending upon our nature and sensitivity, it is often small, petty and trivial words or misunderstandings that can lead to the development of more serious situations. James pondered just how much we utterly depend in a relationship upon a love that can be patient, kind, understanding and most of all forgiving, because of the frailties and imperfections of human nature. Men, especially, can sometimes be nincompoops when it comes to their inability to perceive and accept mood changes in a woman, and on such occasions could respond in some sort of logical fashion, using flippant comments of self-justification as though they have no weaknesses themselves, failing to appreciate sympathetically the deeper feelings of the "gentler sex" and what they are experiencing. Ryan had resurrected this recollection of his wife and her confusion over the Darjeeling Tea incident not out of remorse or regret but as a cherished memory. This helped James to realise that their relationship must have been one of mutual understanding and maturity, so that both parties could be both true to themselves and each other without fear. It seemed they had been able to ride these waves of imperfections in behaviour whenever they appeared, as indeed the storms of life too when necessary!

James enquired further of Ryan and said, "Tell me, Ryan, how is your life now... if I may ask? How are you?"

Ryan remained quiet and thoughtful for a moment, then he looked up, and looking James straight in the eye replied, "Do you really wish to know the truth of how I am?" Determined to say something anyway, he didn't wait for a response but went on to say, "Well, it's like this. You look outside and see that everything in the world is carrying on as usual. Nothing has changed. The birds are singing; children are laughing. This can hurt and make you feel isolated, because you have lost the most precious thing in your life... and you just end up crying. Take this cruise. I see people all around, happy and enjoying themselves. But this easily fills me with sadness, because I cannot share such pleasures with Jenny. It means nothing at all, if she is not here. She would have loved a cruise!" At this last statement, Ryan held back a wave of emotion and bravely continued, "I expect I'll get over it eventually… that is, if it's true that time really does heal all wounds! Well, forgive me. I don't wish to bore you, but you asked and that's how I am feeling at this moment in time!"

James did find it quite unusual to listen to a man speak so freely and openly about his feelings without reservation or embarrassment, but it did not follow that James found the experience uncomfortable. On the contrary, it was refreshing to sit together and speak honestly and without constraint or inhibition. Ryan seemed to be pleased to talk to James about how he felt, and James mostly listened and let him get on with it.

"It's funny, really," said Ryan, "but I keep recalling the words of old love songs from the sixties. Well, some of the words… those that I can remember. I'm afraid with the moods I am experiencing at the moment these old sentimental songs come back to me as though they know how I feel and wish to rub it in!"

Upon hearing this comment about songs from the sixties, James was eager for Ryan to enlarge on this topic, as he knew lots of songs from that period himself. He asked Ryan, "Is there any particular song you're thinking of?"

"Why, yes. It's a song by the Carpenters I think. It goes something like this:

"Why do the birds go on singing…?"

Upon hearing the first line, James joined in with the next:

"Why do the stars glow above?

Don't they know it's the end of the world?
It ended when I lost your love."

And so it was that the pair were singing together, albeit quietly, and helping one another with the words. Those James forgot, Ryan knew. Those Ryan forgot, James knew.

"I wake up in the morning and I wonder,
Why everything's the same as it was.
I can't understand, no I can't understand
Why life goes on the way it does..."

"Yes, I remember that song," exclaimed James in an excited tone. "Very meaningful lyrics in those days! Songs have never been the same since! I find, looking back over our marriage, it has always been the simple things in life that are the most precious – those that cannot be bought with money."

"You're right there," replied Ryan, "absolutely right!"

On sudden reflection James wasn't quite sure where his last statement had come from. Perhaps upon singing the song with Ryan and recalling the old unsophisticated words and feelings that were commonly expressed in songs in those days, it had reminded him of the early years, when he and Juliet had had little money to spare – and yet how very happy they had been!

By then, both gentlemen were simply enjoying reminiscing down memory lane. Ryan went on to say, "And what I would give to be with Jenny again right now this very minute! I wouldn't be bored just to walk around the deck with her and say nothing at all or to do the most mundane things, because being with her was all that mattered." Ryan was clearly on a roll and wanted to talk. He continued further.

"We were satisfied with simple and small things, just as you mentioned before that you and your wife are. What's her name? Juliet, isn't it?"

"Yes. Juliet. I am very fortunate to have a good wife, too," James said. "I agree with all you have said, Ryan. We are exactly the same, Juliet and I. We didn't feel the need either to overindulge in anything. We are happy as well and satisfied with each other. I think we both have been very blessed, Ryan... in fact, very blessed indeed!"

Upon hearing this shared attribute of their respective wives, Ryan lifted up his eyes and gazed at James. As if having just received a revelation, he spoke earnestly, his countenance now somewhat lightened, "You know, James, I never thought of it that way at all. Perhaps I really should start being more grateful for the privilege of having known Jenny for 14 years. Just fancy that a woman like her loved me like she did!" Looking upwards, as if towards Heaven, with shining watery eyes, Ryan added, "I bless you, dear Jenny! I will never forget the life and times we shared together. I know you would wish me to be happy. May God help me to stop dwelling on the past with sadness all the time!"

What an amazing outcome of events!

There followed a natural interlude in the men's discourse together, and they both feasted their minds on happy thoughts towards their other halves. It seemed appropriate to be still in this precious moment of reflection, where a ray of positive hope had seemingly just shone down upon Ryan.

It is true that gratitude and thankfulness can dispel negative feelings by presenting the mind with a positive and entirely different perspective of a matter, an opposite picture of the same situation. Ryan placed his hands around the sides of his face to shield from view his teardrops as they fell for a second time upon the table. This time, however, there seemed to be a different atmosphere upon the moment. If before he had shed tears of sadness, this time they were tears of gratefulness.

"Yes!" exclaimed Ryan, wiping his eyes with a tissue, "You are absolutely right again! I have been very blessed!" He spoke as if he was bringing to conclusion a certain episode of grief in his life and was about to face the future now with a new perspective and focus. After looking down towards his watch and realising that it was approaching 11.00am, Ryan said, "Well, it will soon be time for a photography class for beginners, which I would like to try out. It is a hobby I have always wanted to do but never got round to. Jenny told me several times to start a class if I were really interested. I can imagine her now saying, 'About time, Dear... about time!'"

"Why! That sounds brilliant," said James with an encouraging tone of voice. Then suddenly, their conversation was interrupted by the appearance of Juliet returning from her singing lesson.

"Hi there," said James to his wife. "How did it go?"

"It was very good," she replied gleefully. "I thoroughly enjoyed it, and my friend, Cathy, and I have decided to meet up and go again tomorrow. It is really good. They teach you to sing in harmony!"

"Juliet," James addressed his wife, "meet Ryan. Ryan, this is my wife, Juliet."

Ryan glanced intently at Juliet as he shook her hand, for now he was able to see 'live' the person he had heard so much about. On making this introduction and being aware that Ryan had expressed the desire to leave at 11.00am, James continued to explain to Juliet, "Unfortunately, Ryan is just about to leave to go to a photography session."

Ryan rose to his feet at this convenient and opportune moment; just before leaving, he shook Juliet's hand again warmly and said how very pleased he was to meet her and that he had spent a very profitable time talking to James. Afterwards, Ryan turned to James and shook his hand somewhat more vigorously; looking closely into James' eyes, Ryan said, "Yes, James, we have both been very blessed indeed!"

As Ryan moved away, he turned around and, smiling, lifted one hand to say a second goodbye, "Thank you very much, James. I appreciated our talk very much."

This was the last time James saw Ryan to speak to, but it was not the last time he thought about the other man and the conversation they had shared.

"He seemed to be a nice man," said Juliet, glancing at Ryan whilst he was still in view and wondering with some intrigue what the men had been talking about for so long – and just what the topic of conversation had been in order for such an impression to have been made upon him. "I take it you did not get to the gym."

"No, Dear, I did not. As soon as you left to go to the singing lesson, he came and sat down opposite me and we had a very interesting conversation for almost one hour. I would like to share it with you."

"Okay, My Dear," replied Juliet, "but first I must have a drink."

"That sounds a good idea," James replied. Choosing to sit upon a comfortable settee beside a table, he asked Juliet, "What would you like to drink?"

"Tea please," she replied with gleaming excitement and anticipation at the welcome thought. "A light Darjeeling Tea would be lovely."

"That's good." James smiled thoughtfully to himself at this second request in the space of one hour for this particular brand of tea. Knowing full well what the likely answer would be, he deliberately went on to ask his wife, "With or without milk?"

"With milk please, of course!" Juliet replied with some degree of surprise that James had asked her the latter question for she never drank black tea. Turning and walking over towards the nearby drinks location, James continued to smile and said to himself in a quiet but audible voice, "Well, James, let us hope you get this right!"

The Cottage Flower

One day I stood staring at a vibrant flower growing out of a wall...

Its name is not so important; its description is. Even more interesting is the habitat this particular flower calls home – of all the places to grow, it bloomed in-between two stones on a stone wall!

There happened to be lots of other varieties of plants growing too, but they were mostly very small. This flower that caught my eye was not like all the others. It was large, tall and not just surviving its arid position with seemingly hardly any nutrients, but on the contrary was thriving in its location!

My immediate thoughts were, *How would we like it? Could we thrive and prosper in meek, lowly surroundings and provisions?*

People often believe that when their house is complete and satisfying; when provisions and income are at least adequate, meeting all their physical needs; then they can flourish in happiness and joy very much more than if circumstances were adversely different. At the outset, if the truth is to be known, our expectations towards having a comfortable and happy life are often tempered with false aspirations; so that those things we pursue and highly esteem as providing the perfect remedy for our needs and happiness so often leave us feeling insufficient and still lacking, dissatisfied and even completely unchanged and unfulfilled. Our natural perceptions and understanding of what constitutes a good life are somewhat flawed and so often unreliable.

This flower teaches us a lesson and provides interesting insight regarding the essence of life itself! We will see how it apparently thrives in seemingly adverse circumstances and yet develops far less when conditions are rich in provision and nutrients.

Looking towards an old stone wall at the place where its stone structure met the ground, this specimen grew in abundance. It was a good height of two to three feet tall with a stalky sort of stem that was hollow inside, so that if you bent it far enough, it would snap quite easily with a 'pop.' These stems were quite thick, about half an inch in diameter at their base. Further, the plant had lots of these large stems all bunched together proceeding from the same place at its base. Its leaves were fairly small and of a pale green colour rather than the usual darker green. Mounted towards the head of each stem grew bushy florets of tiny pink flowers bunched together tightly in clusters. The flowers could also be a deeper coloured red or even white.

How this plant seemed to flourish! It was indisputable and spoke for itself. "Look at me and see for yourself!" it seemed to boast. Yet its home was most unexpected and really quite unbelievable, if only the observer were to stop and stare for a while and take it in. Such are the amazing displays of nature – God's handiwork that we grow used to seeing, yet somehow we fail to really observe their incredible beauty!

The plant grew out of a small gap in-between stones, where it was completely stripped of natural resources. *Where was its soil? How could it grow so big in such a position?* There was no sight of a source of the normal requirements of a plant. Yet this flower was not just surviving in its plight or struggling pitifully but was doing so well!

After it had been in flower for a long period of time, it formed its seeds like fluff in similitude to the willow herb found in wasteland. Blowing in the wind they would land in all manner of places. At about this time, the plants needed to be cut back down to the ground in an unmerciful manner only to immediately shoot up again within a week or so and grow vigorously to exactly the same height as before in the same year, bearing the same bushy florets of tiny pink flowers.

Some of the seeds that were randomly scattered abroad by the wind would be seen to grow into tiny new seedlings the following year. Dozens of them, having survived nature's way of sowing, grew here and there. Some seeds fell on healthy soil beds with plenty of nutrients and potential nourishment easily at hand. *Surely they would grow stronger and better here in this environment?* Others were growing in what appeared to be the most inappropriate places amongst stones and gravel, in cracks and corners and on the top and sides of stonewalls in between neighbouring stones!

As the plants grew taller, one would think that this environment would be unfruitful and insufficient for its needs, and that they would wither, not finding sufficient food and water to maintain their height. *They cannot possibly survive or fully grow on the top and sides of a wall,* I thought. It seemed obvious that the most fortunate seedlings were those that were growing in the deep fertile soil, and these would predictably stand the better chance of success. However, the tests of time can reveal many unusual things not at all obvious or to be anticipated!

So often those securities esteemed highly necessary and desirable for a happy life prove to be inadequate in practice, whilst seemingly less favourable conditions and circumstances prove to be far more happy and successful – especially in those things that really matter. In fact, they can often be the most precious times! Why is this? Why is it that one can be so happy sometimes in a simple way of life with limited resources, whilst quite the reverse can happen when provisions are in full supply? We will have opinions and answers to this question, but do we really learn from them? What do we seek as our main priority in life?

It is often said that you cannot have a generous person's happiness if you do not have their generosity. Neither can we have another person's accomplishments and rewards, if we do not do the work they have done to acquire them. When we have no choice but to overcome a difficult circumstance or situation by confronting it, we can learn how to cope with patience, determination and hope, and thus appreciate all that we do have.

Such experiences can often produce strength of character and resilience, two qualities that are frequently diminished with the absence of challenges and trials. In fact it is quite probable that the wisdom and discretion acquired through having to face and overcome challenges in life cannot be obtained in any other way but through these adverse experiences. We cannot easily understand what course of action is required or know what direction to take in a given problem situation, if we have never been challenged by it before in the first place. Necessity has always been the mother of invention.

These thoughts seem to be justified when observing the little seedlings grow in the various places they happened to find themselves. *Which plants would grow the best? Which would develop the strongest roots and stems producing a tall vigorous plant?*

Interestingly, those seedlings in the open, fertile soil grew modestly, as though lacking vigour and strength, and attained only a small to average height. In contrast, those plants that grew in the corners of the wall, in cracks and small openings flourished. They seemingly had developed the ability to adapt to these conditions where food and water were not available in abundance. How they must have dug down deep with their roots to find water and sufficient food!

Nature rewards effort and perseverance; likewise, we have been made to thrive with it and lack without it. Are we not encouraged to seek and to search until we find? To trust with faith and be content remembering always that a person's life does not consist in the abundance of the things they possess? Above all, we are taught not to be anxious or to worry about our life, but to seek first the One who created it – the One Who promises in so doing to add all things that we need, both temporal and eternal!

"For the invisible things of Him from the creation of the world are clearly seen, being understood by the things that are made, even His eternal power and Godhead so that they are without excuse."
Romans 1:20

What is this life if, full of care,
We have no time to stand and stare.
No time to stand beneath the boughs
And stare as long as sheep or cows.
No time to see, when woods we pass,
Where squirrels hide their nuts in grass.
No time to see, in broad daylight,
Streams full of stars, like skies at night.
No time to turn at Beauty's glance,
And watch her feet, how they can dance.
No time to wait till her mouth can
Enrich that smile her eyes began.
A poor life this if, full of care,
We have no time to stand and stare.

W. H. Davies 1871-1940

The
Weeping
Willow
Tree

The Weeping Willow Tree

What a beautiful tree! I thought to myself, as I gazed through the window of my room and observed a Weeping Willow. *So aptly named!*

It stood upon a carpet of pleasant, short, lush green grass near the bank of a narrow, fast-moving river. Nearby was a small wooden bridge that spanned the river; a pathway followed on from it into yet another field. *The beauties of the fresh, untouched green countryside... how picturesque!*

Over the bridge the grass changed its texture to a taller and much more rugged beige colour. The pathway through this wilder grass was winding, as though it sought the most acceptable route until it reached a hedge. Beyond the hedge was another field, and beyond that another, until they touched the distant skyline.

I turned my eyes back again and refocused them on the beautiful tree and the river flowing alongside it. This time I saw a different picture in my mind from the natural one that first greeted me. An equally beautiful scene came to me and spoke of a certain type of person whose character and integrity were just as welcome as the wonderful display of nature before me and perhaps even more so! Yes, it was Psalm 1 that I was drawn to.

"Blessed are those who do not walk in the counsel of the ungodly or stand in the path of sinners or sit in the seat of the scornful but their delight is in the law of the Lord and in His law they meditate day and night. They shall be like a tree planted by the rivers of water that brings forth its fruit in its season; whose leaf also shall not whither and whatever they do shall prosper."

I decided to walk towards the tree and observe it more closely. The branches bowed over as if in obeisance to their creator. They drooped and reached towards the ground, displaying their long garlands of small pointed leaves. Their appearance resembled hanging decorations suspended by strings. The lower ones oscillated like swinging pendulums in the light gentle breeze. *Was this the reason the tree was so called, as if teardrops fell from each drooping branch?*

You are a strong tree, I thought, *with the potential to grow tall and majestic in glory, and yet you bow your branches towards the earth in all lowliness. Had you pointed your branches to the sky instead and not limited your stature by drooping them low, you could have displayed and manifested your true glory for all to see!* In human terms, humility and submission, whenever recognised and respected, have their own beauty. These are qualities that do not seek to parade themselves but would rather seek to address the concerns and needs of others above their own. Simply put, they are unselfish! We can think quite erroneously when we always ascribe greatness to those who seemingly have earthly power and sway, wealth, education or privileges.

As I meditated upon this in a sort of philosophical manner, I was reminded of a certain Person – that great man of history Who, in all His glory, chose also to bow Himself with humility and submission, shed tears and walk this earth in obedience to the will of His Father. One Who could have appeared so gloriously but Who, instead, willingly gave up His glory and power that we might know a God of love, grace and forgiveness! Whenever I think in this direction, an endless supply of verses comes to mind, and I found myself reminded on this occasion of one in particular.

"Though He was a Son, yet He learned obedience by the things which He suffered. Though He was rich, yet for our sakes He became poor that we through His poverty might become rich! Being found in appearance as a man, He humbled Himself and became obedient to the point of death, even the death of the cross!"

Perhaps this tree with its weeping garlands had a special message far more searching than I had first realised! *There is a different attitude and way of thinking here*, I said to myself, *quite different to that of the view of the world at large.* If a Person such as He should choose to surrender all and condescend to human level, then bow before His Father's will as a servant to his master, what kind of message does this speak to me regarding how I should live, if I profess to believe in Him? As if in answer to that question, the next verse came alive in my mind.

"He who says he abides in Him ought himself to walk just as He walked."

Perhaps for the first time I saw a beauty in the state of humble submission to the will of God.

In order to be such a person, I knew I would need to completely surrender to His will and give full devotion to His Word. Then and only then might I begin to understand Him more and comprehend His compelling love that caused Him to utter unselfishly, "Not as I will, but as You will." He would be all I need – my motive, purpose and ambition in life – and not just a religion!

These words of Jesus began to cut with conviction through my current way of thinking, revealing a better way – indeed the only way pleasing to God- for I had thought, being a church-goer, I was doing well. Having a traditional faith in God would surely suffice, and yet why did I not feel so? Why did I feel so empty and dead as though craving a more meaningful purpose to my life? The effects of my zeal and efforts in seeking to do all of the right things were seemingly no more rewarding than anyone who never believed at all; in fact I secretly felt they were much more free and happy than I! *How could this be?* A challenging statement given me a long time previously came back right there and then, "Do you want religion or a relationship?"

Clearly, to be real, I needed to be the person rather than act the person! To know Him personally for myself rather than to know of Him! *Could I freely give to others as I had freely received from Him?* What a place to be in!

There is clearly a strong link portrayed in the Person of Christ between loving God and loving people, so that the first cannot exist in isolation. I cannot love God and not love what He loves! God's love was manifested when He sent His Son to seek and save those who were lost. What a selfish person I am if I simply love only what He gives and provides for me!

I challenged myself under this conviction. In self-rebuke I judged and asked myself, *Have I ever erected a wall of defence over a matter in a self-righteous sort of way and been defiant, standing my ground assuming I was right and the other person was wrong, instead of perhaps dealing more graciously and accepting some of the blame myself? Am I afraid to submit to others when I know I should, but instead retreat out of the fear of being trampled upon or perhaps because I am simply too proud to humble myself before them? Are there any buttons upon my heart that no-one should press lest they release and expose sensitive areas in my life that have not been dealt with and remain as open wounds? Can the doors of my heart be unlocked and opened easily to give unselfish love and blessings to others, or am I like a fountain that is sealed or a spring whose waters cannot flow because it is blocked with the clutter of life? Am I like a garden of scented flowers planted by the Gardener, but through fear hiding away in seclusion, isolation and bondage, afraid to say or do anything? Do I have the freedom and liberty to proclaim aloud and say, "Let the wind blow upon the garden of my heart that its perfume and sweet odours may flow and enable all to smell the fragrance of His Love."*

Am I as free as this? I thought. *Not really. Out of all my profession, what do I really show for it?*

I concluded that if I were to walk as He walked, I would need my priorities to be His. His purpose and will to be mine. To love the things He loved. Agape love! Unselfish! Unconditional! It cost Him His all that we might be forgiven and that we might know Him. Truly it is stated:

"In this the Love of God was manifest toward us that God has sent His only begotten Son into the world. This is love, not that we loved God but that He loved us and sent His Son to die for us. If God so loved us, we also ought to love one another. A new commandment I give to you that you love one another as I have loved you."

As I walked away from the tree and went back towards my room, I knew there was something I had to do. Just as He bowed His head and gave up His Spirit on the cross, I likewise had to go and bow my own head before Him. After all, the Bible is simple and clear when it says,

> "To as many as received Him, to them he gave the right to become children of God. By Grace are you saved, through faith, not of works lest any man should boast; it is the gift of God."

I had previously never considered seeking Him for who He is. I had asked many things of Him but never sought to know Him personally in my life. I trembled when His words flashed through my mind, "Depart from me for I never knew you!"

No service or works could be greater than my personal relationship with my heavenly Father. I realised that I must seek the Giver more than the gift. Within the depths of our being there is a longing for our thirsty soul to be satisfied, and only God Himself can be the answer to this cry. Nothing else will suffice! I could just imagine Jesus when He said,

> "Whoever drinks of this water will thirst again, but whoever drinks of the water that I shall give him shall never thirst."

And again,

> "If anyone thirsts, let them come to Me and drink."

This Person, having put aside His splendour and glory had bowed in submission and humility like a branch of a Weeping Willow tree. Instead of fame, He chose obedience. He had come to do the will of His father. I determined from that day forward to say to myself, *By God's grace, so shall I!*

"My Son; give Me thine heart."
Proverbs 23:26

EDIT the TAPE

Reflections on Life

Edit the Tape

I was sitting before a log fire staring at the yellow flames. The radiant heat warmed my face just like the sun in a clear sky. The flames stretched upwards like dancing, yellow tongues reaching as high as possible and flowing with the draught of air. Wherever the air flowed, the flames followed. The scene captured my gaze easily and effortlessly. The warmth was comforting and relaxing.

Intruding into my mind without invitation were thoughts and meditations of the workday just ending. They began with the first experience of the morning and then gradually moved throughout the day. Each passing moment came like a vivid picture, as though a reel of film had captured all, saved it and was now playing back each scene on the screen of my mind.

Some things had been fulfilling and brought a feeling of satisfaction, a sense of achievement that various tasks had been accomplished that day. I remembered the words of the preacher, "Every person should eat and drink and enjoy the good of all his labour; it is the gift of God!" They became very meaningful words at that moment, for I felt and understood something of the good from my own labours that day.

After this reel had run its course and was exhausted, other older film began to play through my mind – film recorded long ago. It showed memories from the past – some of those memories of times very much earlier than my present day's meditations just relayed and reflected upon. The reel came from the archives, dusty and old, yet able to resurrect unforgotten memories as vividly as though they were yesterday! Times past. Earlier years. Then came childhood and its simple, uncomplicated and unreal world. How different was life's perspective then! How innocent!

A log on the fire tilted on its side causing a sudden burst of yellow flames to eagerly engulf it, feasting upon the unburnt wood now exposed to the red heat. Having distracted me from my thoughts for but a moment, it seemed to speak and say, "Sorry to disturb you. Carry on; we are listening."

Not a care! Not a burden or anxiety was in those simple memories of early childhood! Different sets and scenes like props in a theatrical performance flashed through my mind. There appeared my parents, my family. I could see myself playing as a child in nearby fields close to our home. I remembered the woods by name: Dead Wood, Black Wood and the Spinney. These were my second home. I might be climbing trees or fishing for tadpoles and sticklebacks. What joy in catching one!

I saw the old mission beyond a pathway that went alongside the edge of Dead Wood, which displayed a message in large letters: *SEEK YE THE*

LORD WHILE HE MAY BE FOUND. CALL YE UPON HIM WHILE HE IS NEAR.

Such simple memories were now so very special! "These are the golden years of your life," echoed the voice of my father, his advice making no impression upon me at the time. "They move very slowly now, but in later years they will travel much faster. You will see..."

Oh that all memories could be like these! If only the regrettable and undesirable ones could be cut away from the tape and the two ends of the film spliced back together again without them. Pondering thoughtfully and somewhat philosophically, I asked myself, *What is my life?*

Some of the preacher's words came rushing to the forefront of my mind as if longing for the opportunity to speak. "It is even a vapour that appears for a little time and then vanishes away. Man who is born of woman is of few days and sees much trouble. He comes forth like a flower and fades away." As a child, I imagined I would live forever!

It was during this stupor of reflections of former times that several visitors sought to impose their presence in my mind very strongly. One was called "negativity" and another "melancholy sadness." Both intruded like unwelcome visitors who seemed to thrive upon self-pity and remorse. They had found the perfect opportunity to manifest themselves. Regret and self-pity are never short of memories! They roll forth like oncoming waves on the seashore, then recede back again into the hidden closet of the soul having deposited their debris on the sands of the mind. *I could have done better than I did*, came self-rebuke. *I have failed miserably*, sounded another self-destroying accusation. *You were not good enough*, spoke the voice of low self-esteem. In my own mind, I had every justification for these negative feelings. I would find legitimate reasons for every one of them. Having chosen the course of self-pity, I had found a peculiar sense of comfort in being the victim!

It was whilst I dwelt in this cave of dark despair and self-delusion that I felt the presence of someone nearby. I heard a quiet voice speaking to me, *"What are you doing here? Why are you dwelling in this place?"*

Strong feelings of self-justification flooded into my mind in defence. I replied with some animosity saying, "I was conscientious in life, yet everything I sought to do simply recoiled back at me unfruitfully. I was misunderstood, never given a chance, and now I feel unfulfilled, empty and rejected. I am alone and through no fault of my own!"

Suddenly, there was a sound of a rushing wind approaching me with increasing ferocity. A wind called "illumination." As it blew against my face, my eyes were opened so that I could see and understand certain things about my past that I had never been able to see before. The wind seemed to unfold in my mind some of my motives during those times and those bad experiences when only injustice was pre-eminent in my calculations. I saw, as it were, through a microscope certain things that had been hidden to my observations before. Basically, wherever I had endeavoured to succeed in life, it had been tainted with self-interest or self-glory. There was so much of *self* present!

In such cases, when self is the focus of one's vision, it inevitably brings with it baggage of some kind – baggage so often latent and hidden, but which manifests itself as hurt, inadequacy or failure. They would especially rear their heads whenever the onslaught of difficulties of a personal nature arose.

By now, the winds of enlightenment had gradually subsided, and the personal disclosures they had revealed had come to an end. Its effect upon me was depressing and brought with it even greater despair!

Before I could drown in the depths of these recent revelations, I heard the same voice that had spoken to me before. This time it came as a still, small voice and comforted me with its gentleness. There were no tones of condemnation within its sound but rather empathy and understanding. I listened intently hoping for some sympathy or encouragement. Somehow I intuitively knew that this voice belonged to Someone much higher than me, Someone Who in fact probably knew everything about me! He now spoke to me in a friendly but authoritative and commanding voice, saying pointedly, ***"Come out of the cave where you are*** *dwelling in isolation. Come and stand at its entrance before Me."*

I knew that by being drawn away from my solitary place of isolation and seclusion into the open light I would feel more vulnerable. I felt there was no choice but to go forward and not backward with my life, that things could only improve for me. I knew He would inevitably speak to me again, and I was led into the light of His counsel.

As I wondered what would follow next, He spoke firmly, *"Listen to Me. Hear My instruction and be wise. Do not turn away."*

So often in the past I had withdrawn from confrontations about life's hurts and memories and any attempt to discuss them. I had heard it all before! Yet this voice I had not heard before. It was direct, challenging and spoke to me personally. I needed to know just Who this person was Who gripped my attention in such a compelling manner, so I asked with increasing curiosity, "Who are you?"

"My name is Wisdom," He answered and then continued, *"Does not Wisdom cry out and Understanding lift up her voice? To you I call. My voice is to the children of men! Listen, for I will speak of excellent things. My mouth will speak truth. Whoever finds Me finds life! Take heed and beware of covetousness for one's life does not consist in the abundance of the things he possesses. For naked you came from your mother's womb onto the Earth and*

naked shall you return there. What profit therefore is it to a man if he gains the whole world and loses his own soul? Therefore do not lean on your own understanding. Come and learn to trust in Him with all your heart. Acknowledge Him in all your ways and He shall direct your path.

"Know this truth, that the way of man is not in himself; it is not in man who walks to direct his own steps. There is a way that seems right to a man but its end is the way of death. Therefore, seek first the Kingdom of God and His righteousness and all the things you need shall be added to you. Delight yourself also in Him and He shall give you the desires of your heart! 'What is my life?' you asked. It is a vapour that appears for a little time and then vanishes away. Even the world is passing away and the lust of it... but did you know that he who does the will of God will abide forever?"

My heart burned within me while He spoke to me! "This all sounds so wonderful, philosophical and idealistic for a very young person perhaps who is just starting out in life, but me? How am I able to embrace these truths now?" I cried further, "It is all too late! Far too much has happened in the past! Time and opportunity have deserted me. Things cannot change now. What has been done is done. It cannot be erased. This is my lot."

As if undeterred by all my desperate cries, He continued speaking to me. *"As I said to you before, listen. Listen to Me! To everything there is a season, a time for every purpose under Heaven, a time to be born and a time to die. A time to break down and a time build up again. Now, a time of healing and restoration has come down to you. This is your opportunity if you will receive it; a new season could await you! You did not choose it, neither did you earn it. It is given to you freely. Now is your time! Behold, now is the accepted time. Behold, now is the day of salvation!"*

Overwhelmed by the awesomeness of this experience, I continued in the self-preservation and defence of my pride, thinking to myself, *Why me? Who am I that He should be mindful of me?* Then I cried out, "How is it that you call me and speak to me like this? I am undone in your presence. I have no more answers to offer on behalf of myself. Your words are too much for me to bear; I have no answer to them. I have utterly failed and am unworthy. Why do you speak to me so personally? Can I be of any importance to you?"

He again answered me saying, *"Look at Me and do not doubt; only believe. See My hands and My feet! It is I! Blessed is he whose transgression is forgiven and whose sin is covered. Blessed is the man to whom the Lord does not charge any sin to his account. If man says he has no sin, he deceives himself, and the Truth is not in him. If a man confesses his sins, I am faithful and just to forgive him his sins and to cleanse him from all unrighteousness! Come with Me. I will take you to Calvary. God has granted unto you repentance to life. You must be prepared to change your mind and your thinking as well as the direction of your life. Though your sins are like scarlet, they shall be as white as snow. I am the only One Who is mighty to save to the uttermost all who come to Me. I give life to all who believe on Me!"*

He took me to a hill and there showed me His cross. Why, I cannot say. How, I do not know. But something happened to me! Suddenly, from deep within my innermost being was released a flow of tears like a fountain bursting forth. And as they fell from my eyes, they took within their flow every weight and every burden! I felt clean with an amazing peace. I felt the presence of God! I seemed very close to Him, yet with no fear. What was happening?

Suddenly, the scene changed. The hill and the cross both drifted away from my vision. My eyes met flickering flames from the remains of the log fire before which I sat. Where I had been, what I had heard and seen... I could scarcely tell anyone. One thing I did know is that I had somehow been confronted with my past, and a spiritual change had taken place within me!

All the words of the preacher from my early days had visited me; only this time they had meant something. I understood for the very first time their meaning. I could not believe the transformation and illumination that had somehow taken place within me. A popular song came to me with lyrics that said, *"I once was blind but now I see!"* I get it now!

From that day forth, I knew my dark past was past! A voice often came to remind me, **"Like a thick** *cloud, I have blotted out your sins. The tape of your life has been edited. You are not the same person!"*

As I continued my journey along the path of life, with my feet as light as a feather and a heart intoxicated with joy, I would often catch the attention of people passing by who heard me quietly singing, "I once was lost but now am found, was blind but now I see."

The wonder of it all came to me one day as I read for myself, *"Eye has not seen nor ear heard, neither has it entered the heart of man the things which God has prepared for those who love Him."*

Could there ever be a joy so great and a feeling as wonderful as that I experienced that day? I will always remember the voice of Wisdom when He called me with His words, *"Whoever finds Me finds Life! To you I call!"* I thank God that He did!

Epilogue

The work in producing this book was progressive over several years. The motivation was always to capture life's difficulties, as if taking a photo, its image being firmly planted upon the mind, and then write about each picture as inspired by the Holy Spirit. As previously mentioned at the beginning of this book, only through the compassion of our Lord working in us by the Holy Spirit can we address peoples' hurts and problems and not turn away.

This was reflected when writing *Calvary, Edit the Tape* and *Darjeeling Tea*. The impact upon me was that of a great awesome God of love, grace and compassion Who so desires to release all from sin and set us free.

In some cases I was clearly shown pain and hurt. As a result, it had to be written down on paper! Just as a musician seeks to produce on an instrument the music upon his heart, so I attempted to do likewise with this revelation and compassion of others – but on paper.

God's remedies, as they surged from the endless stream of the Living Word of God, sought to infiltrate what was being written and were applied to their situation as a great physician applying healing balm upon a wound!

Oh the silent suffering, the needless pain carried by so many! And yet *there is a balm in Gilead* that heals the sin sick soul* – a truth written by a thoughtful songwriter and expressed solemnly by Jeremiah for God's people of old.

* Jeremiah 8:22

It was as if God wanted others to read these stories. Their contents describe so many who suffer and experience similar happenings and events in their own lives – silent pain, regretful memories and past mistakes, all of which become hidden burdens and weights that have left their mark. This was captured as an allegory in *Calvary*, but as an actual real life experience brought out in *Edit the Tape*.

If anything, the reader will have been shown that our God is very sensitive to all our feelings and infirmities and always speaks to us for our own good. Never give up on Him! I hope the reader will personally benefit from these stories of encouragement, it being far better for this than merely to read alone. Let each page minister to you as He wills.

Finally, I believe, at this point, it may be relevant and helpful to some to mention that I have personally experienced the traumas of pain through periods of suffering depression, and in the future I intend to publish a fictional novel about this awful and very often stigmatized, misunderstood sickness. This will be portrayed in the life of a beautiful young lady – *Dorothy McGuire* – so watch this space!

I am excited both about this book and the forthcoming novel, which will bless thousands who experience this dreadful condition. Again it is God – the Master Physician – Who knows how to help.

Further, it is my hope to produce yet more stories such as these.

God bless you.

Brian Reddish, June 2015

Lightning Source UK Ltd.
Milton Keynes UK
UKOW07f0713121115